LAW AND CHAOS

The "Stormbringer" Animated Film Project

Text and Illustrations by
Wendy Pini

FATHER TREE PRESS • Poughkeepsie, New York • 1987

For Pa and Dorothy Thomas

Law and Chaos: The Stormbringer Art of Wendy Pini

Published by Father Tree Press, a division of WaRP Graphics, Inc.

Design: Diane Schaefer

Production: Richard Pini

Permission to draw from the ideas and words of Michael Moorcock, as published by the Berkley Publishing Group, is gratefully acknowledged.

Front cover: "The White Wolf." Back cover: "Elric and the Balance."

First Printing November 1987
10 9 8 7 6 5 4 3 2 1
ISBN 0-936861-04-5 (paperbound)
    0-936861-05-3 (lim. ed. hardbound)

Printed in U.S.A.

✳ STORMB

Safeway's paperback book and magazine rack, where newsprint pages absorbed the smells of fresh produce and the coolness of grocery store air, was the lunch-hour haunt of my sixteenth year. I preferred buying comic books there. The only convenient alternative was to walk a few blocks down to the newsstand that fronted Steinmetz's Pool Hall; they usually had the latest titles in stock. Unfortunately their magazine rack stood near the open door to a smoky back room where the pool players could see out better than I could see in.

The vague hint of danger in the men's remarks as I hunted through biker and kinky sex magazines for my favorite Marvel comics was sometimes exciting. Usually, though, I resented the ones making the comments, because any female, attractive or not, would have been the target of their jokes. It was irritating to be lumped, categorized, written off. Boys' cameraderie. Boys' fun.

But the sharks didn't realize that I had already taken many a dip in their forbidden waters. I read science fiction and comics — superhero comics — which was not the usual fare of a girlish go-go booter in 1967. Moreover I liked to draw those trashy, rock-muscled heroes and villains, those male power fetishes. Something male inside me wanted power too. He already had a face.

That year I learned one of his names — *Elric*.

The white face framed in space blue stared out, sphynx-like, from Safeway's paperback stand. That thin, oval mask with its slanting red eyes and delicate chin dominated the cover of *Stealer of Souls*, a newly released American anthology of short stories by English author Michael Moorcock. Intended to lure fans of heroic fantasy with its promise of diabolic sorcery and bloodletting, the title meant something far different to me; my soul had already been stolen, long ago, by those stark kabuki features painted by cover artist Jack Gaughan. It was a face my own hand had drawn countless times with varying aesthetic results, the face of an old friend, companion to darkly imaginative young girls. Demonic muse, Erlking, Pan, gentle incubus, both male and female, haunter of the introverted, the romantically inclined — I recognized him on the cover of that slick paperback, bought it, and absorbed the first story during Mr. Foster's fourth period art class.

RINGER ✳

Blunt, middle-aged Mr. Foster (who did not regard comic books, cartooning or fantasy illustration as art) and I had an understanding. Although he had grudgingly given me "A"s right through my junior year in high school, he made it clear that he did not approve of narrow and intensely focused interests. Mr. Foster believed that an artist should be open to all influences, all techniques, all mediums and all possibilities. That the quality of his own paintings failed, in my opinion, to reflect his ideals did not make those ideals any less valid. But between my unfounded arrogance and suspicious nature, I could not take the man seriously. Youth's motto of the day was "Don't trust anyone over thirty." Hence our understanding. For the most part Mr. Foster left me alone to pursue my interests.

Michael Moorcock's high-wrought, gloomful prose, on the other hand, filled me with the reverence and fierce delight of a disciple. For the first time in my awareness, someone had portrayed "the Haunter" as a glorified adolescent archetype, with all its insecurities, self hatred and fatalism spread like literary acne across page after page. Male though he was, Elric of Melniboné was a character with whom I could easily identify: a sorrowing Gilgamesh with a dwarfish, red-headed Enkidu in tow; or a vengeful Rama beside his more carefree brother Lakshman, battling hideous Rakshasas in the land of demons. The immature hero's (artist's) self indulgent melancholy seemed wholly justified by his unfavorable encounters with capricious gods. I had found a guru in Michael Moorcock and was over-whelmed by his kind responses to my fan letters.

In most retellings of ancient myths and fairy tales little insight is given into the hero's motivations or his emotional reactions to the harrowing trials he must undergo. But Moorcock gives his version of the classic hero cycle a Hamlet-like twist. The stories in the Lancer Books editions of *Stealer of Souls* and the sequel novel *Stormbringer* overflow with angst. Elric's long list of personal frailties and his consequent self pity make the character both alluring and repulsive. He has all the requisite traits of a tragic hero: noble birth, good intentions and a fatal flaw that leads him inexorably to his doom. He does not wield but rather is wielded by the destructive power of his enchanted runesword Stormbringer, which must annihilate all that he holds dear. Yet so much is he the center of his own universe that at one point in the saga the sun itself stands still in the sky awaiting his next decision. Appropriately, the name *Elric*, of ancient Celtic origin, means *king*.

Smitten like *Anne of Green Gables*' day-dreamy heroine, I immediately began to sketch portraits of the Elric character, adding a tall, slim physique to the beautiful and familiar features that Moorcock described. These drawings, done on ditto-master and submitted to amateur publications known as "fanzines" were greeted enthusiastically by fellow fantasy buffs. But soon those single portraits were replaced by detailed color illustrations of entire scenes from *Stormbringer*. An endless feast of psycho-sexual symbolism and metaphysical imagery, Moorcock's works engrossed and inspired me to the exclusion of almost all other subject matter throughout my senior year in high school.

Perhaps I had been getting ready for a grand obsession ever since I was a yard tall, compelled to cover any smooth surface with intricate scribblings inspired by Arthur Rackham, Alphonse Mucha, Erté, Kay Nielsen, Aubrey Beardsley, Hallmark, Astro Boy and Daffy Duck. Today my childhood sketches produce in me a mixture of respect and disgust. There is a self-conscious, imitative quality in even the earliest drawings that suggests the awareness of an audience and a desperation to appease it. Perhaps that lack of originality was so obvious to family and the Gilroy, California public school system that it accounts for the subtle discouragement I sometimes received. But that precocious commercialism, killing the spontaneity that Picasso himself revered as the true genius of children's art, at least shows a strong sense of personal direction. I wanted to be a cartoonist, to have my drawings move, come to life, like Bugs Bunny and Snow White.

A cartoonist always walks between two realities — the world of the senses and what can be called the theater-of-the-mind movie. Cartooning is motion captured on paper — a moment, a sequence plucked out of time and human experience to be held, looked at, nodded over, shared. Communion is the goal and the cartoonist achieves it by translating everyday events, tragic or comic, into readily understood symbols. The viewer and the unruly ink lines viewed are guided by the artist's vision to a point of mutual recognition, to the release of laughter, and sometimes to tears.

Bugs Bunny and Snow White were, to me, visible validation of the two realities I would carry with me right into adulthood. What I perceived, what I experienced in the world of the senses could be interpreted or re-interpreted through drawings. And drawings, I knew, could be made to *move*. That movement, rather than an imitation of the randomness of nature, could be choreographed to the point, to the punch, to maximum effect. I was convinced *that* was the best way to tell a story.

Even before the town of Gilroy had sidewalks my grandmother, Helen Fletcher, was an elementary school teacher. After her retirement her personal library became a treasure trove of the books she had taught from, books that would probably intimidate today's under-read college freshmen. By the age of five I had been exposed to Shakespeare, Kipling, Milton and all the colors of Lang's fairy books. Although the words didn't always make sense, their music thrilled and painted mind pictures. Many of those early editions contained the romantic pre-Raphaelite and Art Nouveau illustrations that introduced me to the concepts of line and composition. But the stories...the stories were everything: friends, teachers, conscience prickers, jesters. And life, the yarn that spun itself daily, was their source. From the pungent yellow mustard weeds that yearly overran my father's plum orchard to the shiny Looff horses on the antique carousel at the Santa Cruz boardwalk, anything, I learned, could become a storytelling device, an actor or a stage setting in the ongoing mind movie.

My drawing style evolved into an unpolished synthesis of Art Nouveau and the line of the Japanese woodblock print. In the mid-1960s when Los Angeles-based comics historian Fred Patten and artists' den mother Bjo Trimble introduced me to *manga* (Japanese comics) I found in that oriental economy a slicker, better realized version of my own approach. Manga hurried my vision along. No other stylistic influence, except for the mannerism of Kay Nielsen, who designed the "Night on Bald Mountain" sequence for Disney's *Fantasia*, is more evident in my early Elric drawings. My firmly fixed association of cartooning with serious illustration led me to think of interpreting *Stormbringer* through the medium of animation.

Had the current, multi-faceted Cal Arts filmmaking program existed in 1970, the story of my higher education might have been far less limp than it is. I did not want to go to college. I wanted to make a movie and marry Richard Pini, the boy I had met through the letters pages of a Marvel comic book. Neither goal carried as much weight with my parents as did the prospect of a college degree. We compromised. I applied to and was accepted by the then very new and experimental Pitzer College in Claremont, California. There, under the sometimes token supervision of counselors, students could actually design their own curricula. Depending on how one chose to take advantage of it, Pitzer, in association with sister colleges Harvey Mudd, Scripps, Pomona and Claremont Men's College, had a great deal to offer. Away from home for the first time, I went a little bit crazy with the freedom.

My chief joy came in gearing all my classes around one major project — *Stormbringer: the Film* — which Moorcock had given me permission to attempt. "By all means..." was his generous phrase, although it is doubtful that he had any idea what the single-handed effort would entail, or just how unfeasible the dream really was. The practical problems were not his and I did not choose to embroil him in them.

Vaguely a liberal arts major, I took classes in film, video, music theory, creative writing, psychology, conversational Italian (to impress Richard's parents back east in Connecticut), astronomy (to impress Richard), drama, painting and, oddly, political science. My half of the dorm room which I shared with a bemused blonde debutante was littered with scraps of paper, paints, color charts, character model sheets, backdrops, records, tapes and magic markers. The perpetually unmade bed became by turns a shelf when the desk grew too cluttered, a work area, and a retreat when things weren't going well. Often I would cut classes to continue working on backdrops. Many times I *went* to class just to escape.

A great deal of encouragement came at that time from the Los Angeles Science Fiction Society, or LASFS, whose members historically have a high tolerance for obsession. Many of the members, including professional writers and artists such as Larry Niven, Jerry Pournelle, David Gerrold, George Barr and Tim Kirk, were quite familiar with Moorcock's writings and were liberal with both their praise and criticism of my as yet unfilmed artwork. Of particular help to me were David Gerrold, who loaned me his animation disc and light board, and George Barr who simply believed that the attempt itself was worthwhile and who gave me helpful advice on drawing techniques and tools.

Looking back, it was difficult for anyone, even Richard, to relate to me except in the context of my *idée fixée*. Embarrassed by the dark, unfeminine and perverse emotions that fueled my imagination, I felt inadequate in my attempts to communicate to others the impor-

tance I placed on the work. Nevertheless, I used people that might have been friends as a cost-free talent pool. Many people at college, students and staff, were interested in helping me, but I was often unappreciative and sometimes came unglued trying to hold too many reins at once. A shadow self always stood apart, observing and muttering, "You're in this over your head." But that awareness was neither as persuasive nor ultimately as real to me as my vision of the completed film. The vision was very strong and, in its ponderous way, approached in logical steps.

"The Tell-Tale Heart," an animated film made for UPA in 1953 by Ted Parmelee served as inspiration and model. Parmelee achieved the illusion of an amazing amount of movement through the clever use of camera angles, zooms, pans, dissolves and multiple exposures. Full Disney-style animation requires a sequence of twenty four drawings per second of film time — a prohibitive amount of work in the case of an independent project done essentially by one hand. While moments of full animation were planned to accentuate certain key scenes

in *Stormbringer*, by and large I expected to use every shortcut and camera trick available to create the impression of action.

By 1971 the screenplay for the movie had gone through several mutations. Initially I had planned to have characters speak actual dialog, necessitating the synchronization of their mouth movements with the voice track. I got as far as one recording session with some volunteer drama students and a professional voiceover narrator, when I learned that the words would have to be broken down into their component consonants and vowels and charted on an exposure sheet which would then indicate the number of frames needed per word.

Richard and I visited Hanna-Barbera Productions in Hollywood and had the good fortune to observe the voicetrack to the then inproduction *Charlotte's Web* being analyzed on special recording equipment and charted on exposure sheets. The cost of such a job done on a freelance basis for a sixty-minute film, we learned, would gobble up many times over the small grant I had received from Pitzer. Seeing that animated dialog would prove too costly and time-consuming, I re-did the script to tell the story through voice-over narration, sound effects and a classical music score. The timing of scene changes with the narration would be accomplished during the editing phase. Moorcock's labyrinthine tragedy, at once elegiac and bitterly ironic, had to be pared down to what I considered to be an hour's worth of its spiritual meaning.

The work came hard. I was deeply concerned with doing justice to Moorcock's creation and plagued by as much self doubt as Elric ever expressed. In fact, I over-identified with the albino martyr, lived more in his world than in my own. I had no commercial aspirations for the film after its completion. Rather, I assumed that it would be shown and appreciated only at science fiction conventions and club meetings. That didn't matter. The work was being done for me, for Brahma, for the hell of it and as a tribute to a piece of fiction that had touched me more deeply than anything I had previously experienced.

Late in 1971 my short college career began to fizzle out. I'd exhausted my grant and had only a few minutes of poorly exposed 16mm animation to show for it. My grades were unimpressive, I had a couple of incompletes, and the girls in the office ragged me about my records which were not only a shambles but also unfilable. However, there was one bright spot of success. In TV class I produced and directed a video based on the "Pirate Jenny" number from Berthold Brecht's *Threepenny Opera*. The song, interpreted on a phono album by Judy Collins, contained the same sort of cheerful revenge fantasies found in scenes from *Stormbringer*.

"Jenny" was a trial piece drawn and photographed in black and white which took advantage of the class's two video cameras' capabilities. Several other students and I filmed it in one afternoon, using fade-ins, fade-outs, zooms, dissolves, double images, and we even created cannon flashes by burning to white. The results were judged worth an "A". It was a small triumph that I should have taken more seriously, but back then video recorders were not available to the general public and tapes were hard to store. I later learned that "Jenny" had been erased by another student's project a few days after it was recorded. The artwork, somewhat damaged, still exists in my files.

I left Pitzer in the spring of 1972, moved back east and married Richard, who was about to graduate from the Massachusetts Institute of Technology in June. We were both just 21. *Stormbringer* came with me, even though I had lost contact with Michael Moorcock and was finally beginning to lose enthusiasm for the project. The time for a difficult decision was rapidly approaching: finish a labor of love begun in my teens, no matter how long it took, or set aside the things of childhood and assume the responsibilities of marriage and earning a living. Vocally, and not without justification, Richard let it be known that he no longer wanted Elric sleeping between us. The project became the source of many bitter arguments.

Even so, nearly two more years passed before I could completely give up my obsession. To this day the Haunter still visits me from time to time, perching on my shoulder and whispering me toward yet another Sisyphean task. I listen with an educated ear. ✳

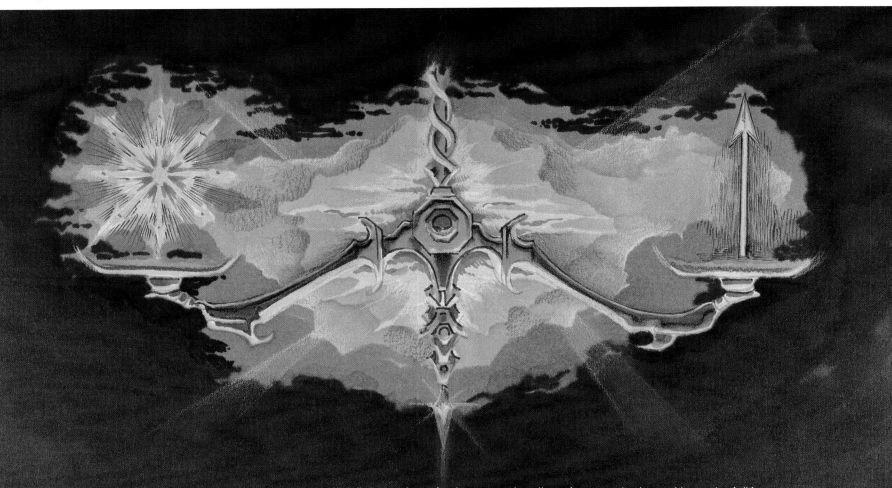

Since *Stormbringer* was a kind of term paper officially begun in my freshman year in college, I expected to be working on it a full four years, which hardly seemed time enough. In my film class I had access to photographic equipment including a 16mm Arriflex camera which was capable of the various special effects I wanted. But I had never used a stop-motion camera before and my first experimental attempts at animation yielded crudely overexposed footage. Somewhat intimidated, I concentrated in the first months on pre-production, screenplay, storyboards, and assembling sound effects and music. It should be noted that this was not done in an organized way and that I carried much in my head that never made it to paper.

Hundreds of drawings had to be churned out, while the medium in which they were rendered had to convey the color and decorative design I wanted. The jewel-like tints of analine dye markers and felt tip pens shaded with Prismacolor pencils proved the happiest and least expensive combination; I could work with them very fast. But the fumes from the markers were noxious and to this day I would not recommend that any artist plan a long term project utilizing them. Subconsciously aware of the health hazard, I was nevertheless very pleased with the transparent colors and delicate detail that blending the markers could achieve.

The novel Stormbringer is divided into four parts, the first of which is entitled "Dead God's Homecoming." In the course of five years this section was the one I translated most heavily into visuals. It will be described here, scene by scene in the present tense, as though it had actually been filmed.

The movie opens with a series of still images depicting the events which shaped Elric's life up to the point where the action begins. This flashback lasts about five minutes with the voiceover narration timed to every nuance of the background music. "Night," a selection from *Scythian Suite, Opus 20* by Prokofiev was such an ideal mood setter that the piece actually influenced the pictorial subjects and the amount of screen time given to each shot. I spent many hours searching out just the right passages to underscore specific scenes. The music and atmospheric sound effects were, in fact, almost as important to me as the art.

Closely following the imagery in Moorcock's description of the declining Bright Empire, I used Russian and Oriental influences in the design of the city of Imrryr the Beautiful and its decadent inhabitants the Melniboneans.

Through the use of cutouts, ominous animated clouds slide behind the buildings as the camera pans across the wide establishing shot.

I was truly the product of a small town upbringing; my brushes with degenerate behavior had amounted to one or two harmless passes from a lecherous history teacher and a few leers from my "friends" in the back room at Steinmetz's. Since there was not much life experience to draw on, my notion of flamboyant decadence came from films such as *The Fall of the Roman Empire*, *Spartacus*, and even those godawful cheap Italian muscleman flicks with titles like *Ursus Versus the Cyclops*. A 1969 publicity spread in Life magazine on Fellini's *Satyricon* made a strong impression on me. It was Fellini's juxtaposition of extreme beauty with extreme ugliness and the sense that ugliness and decay would prevail which cued the morbid mood I wished to establish visually in *Stormbringer*.

Wanting the audience to feel my own nostalgia for what the Bright Empire must have been like in its golden age, I portrayed the early Melnibonéans as a sophisticated race of High Elves, enjoying the fruits of their intellect and their passions. It seemed logical that after ten thousand years no element of their environment, including their clothing, would be without intricate ornamentation. The older a society gets, the more it whittles away at its own foundations, collapsing when over-decoration turns to decay.

Moorcock's many mentions of the casual cruelty of the Bright Emperors conjured images from DeMille's *The Ten Commandments* wherein godlike Egyptians oppressed the enslaved Israelites. Only in *Stormbringer*, it was the sadistic Melnibonéans who made pacts with demons to terrorize and subjugate the infant human race.

One of the earliest drawings of Elric, predating the commencement of the film by at least a year establishes him as an effeminate but nevertheless imposing character. He is clearly not human, a fact which his albinism emphasizes. He is bejeweled and carries himself with the hauteur of a king from a long line of kings. He is designed to make women's mouths water. The sword, much simplified later in its final representation, has a batwing crosspiece, the curves of which suggest claws, fangs, and all things hurtful and evil.

Elric was a restless king seeking a better way of life for his people who refused to acknowledge their own decline as the human race ascended.

Last of the Bright Emperors, he sits on his ruby throne, contemplating a bleak future. The white whippet is a visual echo of the albino's own paleness and seeming physical frailty.

In Elric, Moorcock created an extremely complex and ambiguous character torn between the lure of tradition and the desire for growth and change. A sorcerer, warrior, philosopher and rebel, Elric sometimes heeds the blood-call of his forefathers and indulges in their torturous pastimes. At other times he bitterly disappoints his people by not being cruel enough.

◄ Ultimately, Elric impressed me as a fellow who, in defiance of Fate, would have preferred spending his life pottering around his arcane laboratory and studying ancient scrolls. Such was the impression that I wanted to give to the audience as well.

In an invented scene, Yrkoon, Elric's wicked and ambitious cousin, exhorts him to punish two humans while Elric's friend and manservant Tanglebones pleads with him to be true to his heritage. ▼

18

◀ The unfinished ballroom scene in which Elric's lady, Cymoril (▶), approaches the throne with her honor guard always tickles me. It is an unintentional satire of a similar scene from Disney's *Cinderella* as shown in the Simon and Schuster storybook I loved as a child. Note the fellow showing his snake to an interested lady in the foreground — hardly subtle! Without question the Disney approach to background and layout, particularly the work of Eyvind Earle on *Sleeping Beauty,* was a strong influence. Upward sweeping, gothic lines help create a sinister mood.

My handwritten directions read: "Ballroom scene — camera slowly PANS from throne to Yrkoon and his cronies."

Cymoril's love was the only thing that made Elric's life as emperor bearable.

◄ Even though the perspective on the curving back wall of Elric's library is noticeably off, I like this still shot because it really evokes the "otherwhere and otherwhen" of Melniboné. The picture has a mat board backing except for behind the stained glass window, which is a cutout. Analine dyes are literally that; they soak through and dye the paper fibers. By backlighting this shot the translucent colors of the window could be made to glow as though sunlight was streaming through.

► Eventually Elric abdicates, leaving his evil cousin Yrkoon to run things in Imrryr. The albino becomes a wanderer dressed in outlandish garb, seeking knowledge of the world the humans are building beyond the Dragon Isle of Melniboné. But the terrible power of his black sword Stormbringer begins to possess him, to bend his mind out of shape. With his human army he returns to Imrryr the Beautiful, intent on razing it to the ground to make way for the new age.

◄ Cymoril dies on Stormbringer's point, a victim of Elric's berserker madness. Here he sets fire to her bedcurtains, his stance revealing as much shame as sorrow. By filming the scene in its actual colors and then slowly dissolving to the same shot photographed through a red gel (▼), the consuming heat of the funeral pyre is suggested.

▲ Leaving his betrayed people, his army and his dead love behind, Elric sails away from the burning Dragon Isle to meet his fate in the world of humans. After completing this still I realized how shortsighted I was to include the ghostly image of Cymoril in the painting. Through superimposition she could have faded in and out of the shot like a dying dream. Constantly I needed to remind myself that my mind was not the camera and that skipped steps meant missed bets.

An outlaw, hated by his own people and by humankind as well, Elric finds himself in a continuous struggle for survival. More and more he comes to depend on the strength Stormbringer gives him as it drinks the souls of those it slays. A far cry from the ancient Bright Emperors who flew their dragons into battle and conquered the world, Elric leads the life of a thief and hired killer, never daring to love or trust others lest they too should fall prey to Stormbringer's hunger.

There is, however, one exception. Gilgamesh had Enkidu. Rama had Lakshman. Don Quixote had Sancho Panza —

— and Elric has Moonglum.

A sturdy, good-humored ladies' man, Moonglum of Elwher fills the classic role of hero's companion.

26

Moorcock's description of the little human could not provide better visual contrast with tall, ascetic Elric. Though Moorcock sometimes refers to Moonglum as ugly, a broad mouth and a bulging nose can have their own appeal. And certainly Moonglum's squat body was easier to animate than Elric's.

To this day longtime Disney animators complain about having had to draw "the damn prince," referring either to the limp, nameless hero in *Snow White* or Prince Phillip in *Sleeping Beauty*. The realistic motion of characters with normal human proportions is very difficult to achieve, even by rotoscoping and tracing live action footage. The rounder and squashier a character's design, the more lively and exaggerated his actions can be.

My interpretation of Moonglum is not entirely successful. To my eye, now, he looks stiff and awkward as though I had attempted to give a tall, thin body's range of motion to a character with a short, stocky physique.

MOONGLUM

Moonglum should have been rougher and more loosely sketched. But mine was a problem that I have seen crop up time and again in the portfolios of aspiring young female cartoonists or comic book artists. Girls soothe the lines they draw, smoothing them down as though carefully making beds. A fine feminine eye for aesthetic detail proves limiting when a character *should* be drawn massively. It's a difficult phase that young women cartoonists in particular go through when having to caricature male anatomy. Often they excel in line, but not in structure. In my case, working on *Stormbringer*, I hadn't evolved beyond my desire to make everything at least a little pretty.

Be that as it may, Moonglum was a delightful character to work with, since he provided not only physical but also emotional contrast to the brooding Elric. Like Orlando and Rinaldo in the centuries-old Italian puppet play *Orlando Furioso,* the saintly hero and his rakish sidekick are two sides of the same coin, two facets of the same personality. ▶

◀ Elric and Moonglum roved the land as freebooters and thieves and their brotherhood seems, for once, stronger than the threat that soul-hungry Stormbringer poses.

30

◄ Tortured by guilt for all the lives he has unwillingly destroyed, Elric always verges on madness. The black sword owns him. He can not throw it away without becoming something worse, in his own mind, than a kinslayer. Without Stormbringer's sorcerous strength flowing through him, Elric's albinism coupled with other degenerative factors leave him weak, helpless, less than a man. Despite the horror and self-hatred all his crimes inspired, Elric fears more than anything the loss of his manhood. The obvious Freudian symbolism — sword equals male potency — interested me less as a filmmaker than the concept of Elric as metaphor for artist.

Since the 1960s American society in particular has regarded the process of artistic creation through mass media blurred eyes. Today in the nightmarish Theater of Imagination at EPCOT Center in Disney World one learns that "creativity is fun," "creativity is easy," "anyone can be creative," and "have a nice day — or else!" My personal experience at age twenty was that the source of creativity was pain. It was compulsive-addictive behavior borne of the need to wrench order from spiritual chaos. I'd love to see a cute lavender audio-animatronic dragon wrap its cute plastic lips around *that*.

I identified strongly with Elric because I saw in him an outsider by choice who could not stop feeling sorry for himself. The black sword represented the creative force, the spark, the gift that brings suffering and loneliness along with joy. No artist with functional talent and the compulsion to express it would willingly throw it away, any more than Elric could cast Stormbringer from him — that is, unless some other, more enticing form of addiction took its place.

In their monomania, creative people often hurt and alienate those closest to them. Guilt may sting them from time to time, but ultimately the obsessed ones feel justified because they are in the grip of something stronger than themselves, something, they claim, that belongs to the world. Only those with egos stable enough to stand alone can love such self-centered and yet curiously uncentered personalities. In keeping with the symbolism which I felt Moorcock had built around those truths, Moonglum of Elwher was, for Elric, one such faithful love. ▼

The Lady Zarozinia of Karlaak, City of Jade Towers, was another (page 33).

In the time-honored tradition of heroic fantasy, Elric meets Zarozinia in the woods while rescuing her from a "fate worse than..." Human, and of noble birth, the lady's most interesting quality is her unflappability. To be sure, the "thunderbolt," or what I would later call "Recognition," strikes Elric and Zarozinia at first sight (pages 32 & 33). But she immediately proves herself stronger than most of the women Elric has known — strong enough to make him forget his misgivings and take one more chance on love.

ZAROZINIA

Sensible, self-assured and warm, Zarozinia's personality paints a better picture of the woman than Moorcock's sketchy physical descriptions do. She is, also in the time honored tradition, supposed to be beautiful. But in my character designs I chose to give her an earthy quality, the opposite of ethereal Cymoril.

Long chestnut hair and a not exactly ravishing face lend Zarozinia an open, approachable air, the very qualities that would draw someone as skittish as Elric to her. She is sensual, a dancer. There might have been the equivalent of hot, Latin blood in her ancestry.

◄ The wedding — one of my favorite stills from the film. Elric marries Zarozinia in her city of Karlaak and settles down there, despite the unease of the general populace.

What I was after in the depiction of the marriage ceremony (which was not described by Moorcock in the *Stealer of Souls* anthology) was a celebration with somber overtones.

Stormbringer has been locked away in the city armory and Elric now maintains his strength with new drugs he has discovered. The silver sword he holds is twined with flowers symbolizing peace. Zarozinia's gown, after an illustration by Rackham, is spring green suggesting a new beginning. The couple joins the old world with the new as their lifeblood mingles, representing the physical and spiritual bond, but also, unhappily, foreshadowing pain to come.

Earlier designs for the wedding costumes, again predating the film, were even more elaborate than those finally chosen. Daydreams about my forthcoming marriage to Richard, I must admit, made costume and character design the most enjoyable aspects of planning the film. ►

Zarozinia wears quilted white leather trimmed in fox fur. Her necklace is jade and her eyes are decorated (in anticipation of the punk movement) with feathers. Elric's collar and tunic front are inlaid with jade set in silver.

38

The flashback is done. The story begins.

◄ As the final notes of "night" fade away a new tune played on a strange musical instrument rises in volume, blending with the background chirr of crickets. The camera slowly zooms into a peaceful, nighttime scene. This is Elric and Zarozinia's home in Karlaak. The palace has been in her family for hundreds of years and part of its wall is broken, revealing a walking area and a balcony.

A light in the window of a cantilevered tower flickers warmly, another backlighting effect. ►

More content than he has ever been in his life, Elric sits behind the great carved wooden desk in his library and seems ▲ finally healed, at peace with the world. His attention, however, is not on his reading, but on the soft music being played offscreen.

I enjoyed drawing Elric with a smile, since he does it so rarely throughout the story. His facial expression in this close ▶ shot is quite successful because the eyes are still a little haunted. However, this shot also taught me a lesson. I wanted the eyes to blink once or twice and thought it would be neat if the rest of him were realistically shaded while only the eyelids moved. So I animated the closing eyelids on clear acetate cels. But when they were overlaid on the finished drawing, the effect looked terrible! Elric's red pupils showed through the acrylic painted eyelids and the expression was spoiled. I needed that little slap to make me realize the separate limitations of illustration and animation. Illustration can be subtle and intricately detailed because it is static. Cel animation must, of necessity, be more broadly drawn, inked and painted. The two approaches do not mesh convincingly in the representation of a single character.

◄ The music which has so captured Elric's attention is Zarozinia's. She is plucking an improbable stringed instrument — should it be called a harpsiloom?

I remember searching in vain through the Scripps music library for an appropriately offbeat string-percussion piece to use during this scene. Finding nothing exactly right, I lugged my tape recorder, a twenty-pound "portable" reel-to-reel, over to the baby grand piano in my dorm's living room. Never quite in tune, the piano sat mostly ignored by serious music students. But I was looking for an off-key melody for Zarozinia to play anyway, and so I fooled around until I managed to hunt-and-peck one out. After several run-throughs, I recorded the tune playing it slowly, then played it back at fast speed. The result was a "plinketty-plunk" sound something like a harpsichord, but weird, and suitable for my needs.

◄ Zarozinia projects total love and trust in this reverse angle shot as she reacts to Elric's gaze. Her background music fades up, the delicate good-night in the closing minute of the "Balcony Scene" from David Diamond's program music for *Romeo and Juliet*. The voiceover narrator informs the viewer of the characters' thoughts as the action proceeds.

Elric blows out the candle as he and Zarozinia prepare to go to bed. She is part of the background but he, painted on a separate cel, slides into the frame from the right. An animated flame flickers and the picture goes suddenly black. This shot was test-filmed using paper cutouts for the guttering flame.

It has been almost twenty years since I began *Stormbringer*, yet there are certain sections of the work that, as an artist today, I am still very proud of, particularly some full color cel animation of Zarozinia mouthing the words "You compliment me overmuch, my lord." Although the few frames of test footage are badly overexposed, Zarozinia does seem to come to life. It is difficult to describe the thrill of flipping a bunch of pencil drawings by hand and seeing your character nod, smile, blink and speak. Imagine how much more exciting it is to see the finished product in action on screen. My reaction, I recall, when I viewed the footage for the first time in film class was an hysterical "It works! She's moving!"

◄ The couple embrace outside their bedroom door. Elric is afraid his happiness cannot last. Zarozinia tries to reassure him. The image slowly spins as the camera zooms out.

▲ A very early line drawing of Elric and Zarozinia. The beard was saved for later in the story.

48

◄ The scene changes to the most complex background in the film, a view of Karlaak through the open city gate. At either side of the frame a guard sleeps, knocked out by a sorcerous spell. Thunder rumbles. The music has switched from "Balcony Scene" to "Lento" from the first movement of Cesar Franck's *Symphony in D Minor*, what I call good sneaking-up music. Recently I was amused to hear it used in an episode of Hanna-Barbera's animated series *Smurfs*.

In this shot the camera becomes an actor, panning first right, then left, then slowly trucking up the road that leads to Elric's palace on the hill. A few frames contain white highlights painted on cels to suggest flashes of lightning. The audience sees all from the point of view (POV) of whatever menacing thing it is that creeps along the road. ►

The music builds its mood of suspense as we dissolve to Elric and Zarozinia's bedroom.

In this complicated shot (page 50 & 51) the camera, still playing the sinister invader, slowly zooms in on the sleeping pair while storm clouds roll past the large bedroom window and lightning flashes illuminate their bodies. The effect is achieved through a combination of cel overlays and sliding paper cutouts. Suddenly there is a great CRASH of thunder and the screen whites out completely. In the next brief shot (page 52) we see Zarozinia's terrified face. She screams. Thunder crashes and the screen whites out again.

A victim of the same evil spell which laid low the hapless guards, Elric sleeps through all this, waking just in time to kill a hideous demon whose companions have already fled. The forces of Chaos have stolen the one thing in the world that matters most to Elric — his beloved wife. Realizing this, he screams his rage at the heavens. ▶

Elric is forced onto the road of destiny once more. Only one thing will give him power enough to combat the gods of Chaos: Stormbringer, his hated, enchanted runesword. Swathed in a black cloak, he goes to the armory where the sword seductively calls to him.

▲ Once again utilizing paper cutouts, the armory door slides open revealing Elric in black silhouette. The camera pans right and zooms into the dark cave where Stormbringer is kept. As the screen fills with this darkness we hear the weird, metallic moaning of the sword. This sound effect was borrowed from the electronic "sound patterns" composed by Desmond Leslie for the Living Shakespeare album of *Macbeth*.

Highlights of the next scene, underscored by a spooky passage from Francis Thorne's *Rhapsodic Variations for Piano and Orchestra*, are detailed here in six panels from a color storyboard, a shot-by-shot camera and director's guide, much like a comic book.

Household servants gather around the dead demon in Elric's bedroom (upper right.). The sorcerer himself returns (lower right.) and orders them out of the room. Alone with the demon, Elric closes the shutters (page 55, upper left). He lights a brazier (lower left) and begins singing a sorcerous incantation to raise the demon (upper right). The demon returns to life (lower right) just long enough to say that Elric must travel west with a kinsman and enter a mysterious bargain with a dead god.

Elric sets out at once on his quest to regain Zarozinia. During this and the following scene the music is from the second movement, "Allegretto" of Franck's Symphony in D Minor. I perceived martial undertones in the lovely, measured harp chords and in the oboe counterpoint, an appropriate aura of purpose and urgency.

Along the way Elric sees much evidence of war brewing in the human lands; he senses that a great upheaval in the order of nature itself is imminent. A forthcoming cosmic battle between the gods of Chaos and the Lords of Law is reflected by the fomenting discord on earth.

◄ Coming to a burned forest, Elric meets a cheerful old hag who has sold her soul to Chaos in order to survive the wars. She (or perhaps he) prophecies that Elric will find his cousin, Dyvim Slorm, in the city of Sequaloris.

Filmed against a dismal backdrop of charred trees, the hag needed to stand out despite her somber-hued clothing. Two possible color schemes were painted on a test cel, but I can't recall which model I settled on.

◄ Elric does indeed find his cousin, Dyvim, who has also received a prophecy — from a talking falcon. According to the bird, Dyvim and his band of Melnibonéan mercenaries must join the army of Queen Yishana of Jharkor. Her enemy, an ambitious human wizard named Jagreen Lern, seeks to conquer the world and has made unclean pacts with evil gods to enhance his army's power. Only sorcery can combat sorcery, and if Elric is to save Zarozinia he must first take on the upstart wizard Jagreen Lern.

An unfinished group reaction shot shows that the Melnibonéan mercenaries, last survivors of the genocide instigated by Elric, are hardly happy to see their emperor again. Their armor has a Spanish flair; its alien elegance is suggested by the contour rather than the interior detail of the drawing. ►

Designing Dyvim Slorm presented some interesting problems. Both his blood kinship with and his personality differences from Elric had to be obvious at a glance. Moorcock gives little physical description of the character other than the honey color of his hair. But that small hint helped me with the overall design. In contrast with Elric's basically cool palette, Dyvim wears warm colors; he is truly one of the "Golden Folk." Comparatively youthful, brash and arrogant, Dyvim embodies all that is left of the careless lifestyle and fatalistic philosophy of the Melnibonéans. He holds no grudge against Elric and is ready for a good battle.

An early interpretation from 1969 of Elric in traveling gear drawn in brown ballpoint pen. The sword is far too short; Stormbringer, like many a medieval broadsword seen in museums today, measured at least five feet from pommel to point. But for the sake of composition, I was often forced to fudge on the length of the blade. Moorcock mentions in the *Stormbringer* novel that Elric sometimes wore the runesword scabbarded across his back. Yet there were times when a hip draw was also indicated. Having spent a couple of years as a dilettante member of the Society for Creative Anachronism (an organization originally founded by folklorists and students of medieval history and culture to faithfully recreate the pageantry of those times) I had observed mock jousts and broadsword duels enough to have some idea of the basic stances and movements of swordsmen.

From the reunion in Sequaloris the scene changes to the encampment of Queen Yishana's army in the valley of Sequa. The music also changes form "Allegretto" to the lively, expectant "Dance of the Young Kurds" from the *Gayne Ballet Suite* by Khachaturian. So enchanted was I by this composer's work that I remember getting into a heated debate over its merits with a gentleman in the Scripps music library. Only after he left did the amused librarian inform me that the man was Gail Kubik, who had scored the Oscar-winning animated cartoon *Gerald McBoingBoing.*

Awaiting Elric's arrival in her tent (page 62), Yishana anticipates renewing her old love affair with him and winning the war with his sorcerous aid. Aging but sexy, an intelligent, bitchy amazon, the warrior Queen of Jharkor is one of Moorcock's most interesting and amusing characters. I envisioned her with Middle-Eastern features, dark-skinned and tall.

63

"How goes your marriage?" Yishana asks the albino sorcerer when he arrives. "Well," he ironically responds. "And now I'm disappointed," she smiles.

▲ Her pasted-on gold foil jewelry was an experiment in light and texture that probably would have proved distracting onscreen.

▶ Obsessed with finding Zarozinia and irritated at this interruption of his quest, Elric ignores Yishana's advances. Both leaders settle down to firming their battle plans. Dyvim Slorm (page 65), in a rare moment of concern, worries about lovesick Elric's ability to think rationally and command the combined army of six thousand troops.

64

Little art for the battle of Sequa actually exists. A montage of imagery filled my mind, but I was overwhelmed by the task of ordering it all on paper. In his lengthy description of the warriors, their weapons, their preparations, and the first encounter of Elric's and Jagreen Lern's troops Moorcock dwells on gory details with ghoulish glee.

As with other difficult sequences, finding the right piece of music to underscore the battle helped me begin to organize my thoughts. The short, violent "Evil God and Dance of the Pagan Monsters" from Prokofiev's *Scythian Suite Opus 20* suited perfectly for reasons beyond its title. As for the din of war, record albums then available for use in radio plays and such contained only contemporary sound effects. So I turned once again to Italian muscle-man movies, recording long, noisy segments of primitive combat off the television in my dorm's living room. The sound quality was poor, full of hiss and static, but with music and narration dubbed over it, I hoped it would pass.

► Sallow and aquiline, Jagreen Lern is a villain of the "Ming the Merciless" school. Whereas Elric's physiognomy suggests the dual aspect of his nature, sinister inhumanity blended with beauty and spirituality, Jagreen Lern's expression is far more predatory, his features harder and less intelligent.

In the midst of the larger conflict surrounding them, Elric and Jagreen Lern meet and size each other up. With all confidence Elric engages the wizard in single combat only to discover that Lern's armor and shield are enchanted. Nothing can penetrate them, not even Stormbringer. ▼

I kept the design of Elric's war gear very simple, as I expected to use him in a couple of fully animated sequences during the battle scenes. Clothing that fits close to the body is easy to draw repeatedly. That's why comic book superheroes always wear leotards.

▶ The first sequence is a simple walk cycle of Elric on horseback, supposedly reviewing his troops. The animation is limited in the sense that Elric and the horse were to be painted on separate cels, Elric's movements requiring a shorter and more frequently repeated cycle than the horse's. The second sequence is an ambitious but amateurishly realized piece of business, only key drawings and no in-betweens, in which Elric wrestles a warrior's horse to the ground, stealing it for his own use.

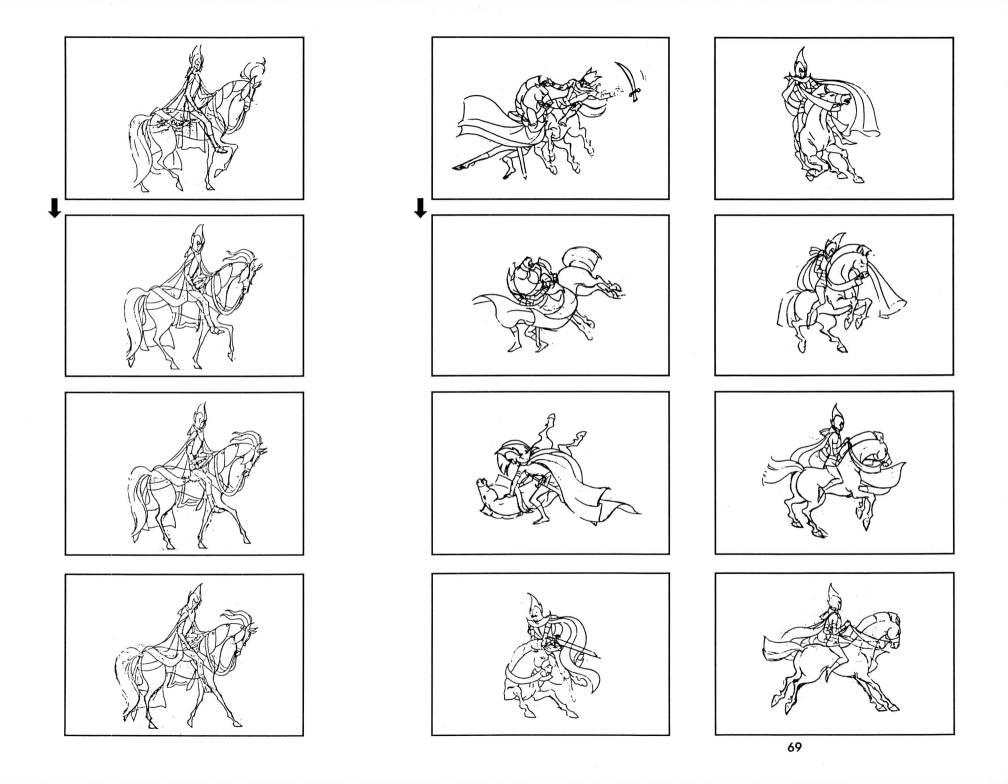

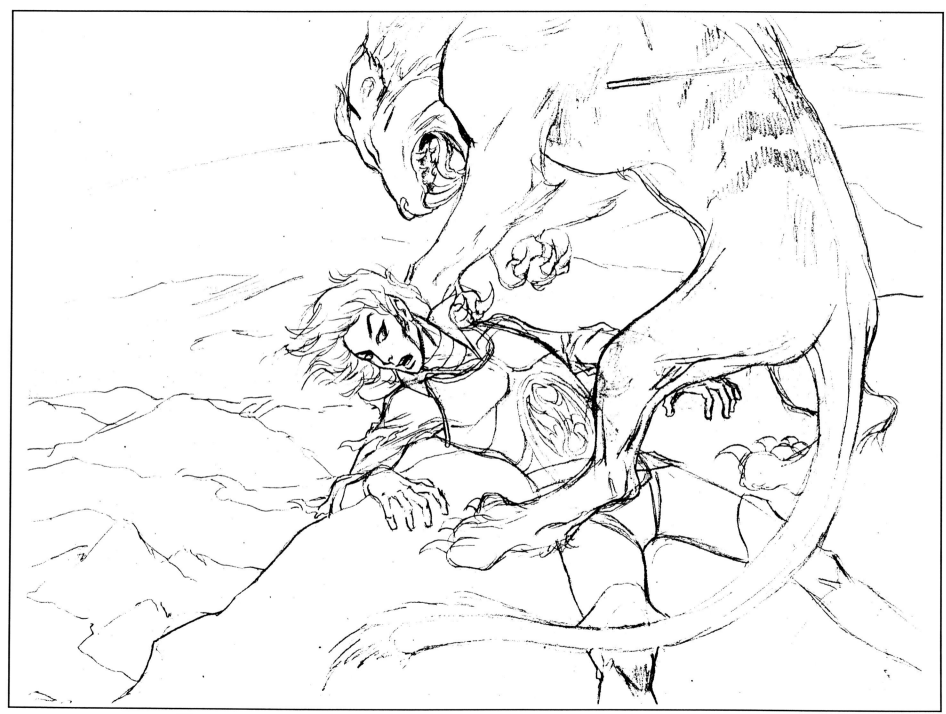

Eventually the tide of battle turns against Elric and Yishana's forces who cannot withstand Jagreen Lern's sorcerous allies. Elric and Dyvim, pursued by great demon cats(◄), are forced to flee high into the mountains. The kinsmen are rescued in the nick of time as two mighty arrows sing through the night air, slaying the monsters. ►

◄ A series of mystical, descending notes from the *Scythian Suite,* "Invocation to Veles and Ala," introduces Sepiriz, Elric and Dyvim's rescuer. Sepiriz, an immortal seer who dwells in the Chasm of Nihrain, announces that he has the power to help Elric find Zarozinia. Not without suspicion, Elric and Dyvim follow the mysterious stranger down into the chasm.

Visually, Sepiriz is Elric's polar opposite, black as ebony, muscular and square-boned. Only his eyes hold a sadness similar to Elric's, for Sepiriz knows the destiny of the albino sorcerer — a destiny which Elric only suspects.

74

◀ In the seer's quarters, deep in the bowels of Nihrain, Sepiriz presents Dyvim Slorm (for some reason drawn here in awkward perspective compared to Elric) with Mournblade, Stormbringer's exact twin. Sepiriz tells the astounded cousins that the black runeblades were forged eons ago to destroy a group of powerful beings known as the "Dead Gods." These gods were hurled into another dimension but one of them, Darnizhaan, has now returned to earth.

▶ In extreme closeup Sepiriz's animated eyes narrow to slits as he reveals that Darnizhaan has kidnapped Zarozinia and will release her only in exchange for the two swords.

The music of Prokofiev fades beneath the agitated opening notes of the fabulous *Schertzo Fantastique* by Ernest Block. Of all the musical passages I pieced together for *Stormbringer's* score, this one pleased me most. It literally tells the story of the dead god's fall.

Knowing that he dares not surrender the power of the runeblades to evil Darnizhaan, Elric hurries with Dyvim to the Vale of Xenyaw where the god awaits them.

Darnizhaan proves to be a jolly and persuasive fellow, inspiring Elric and Dyvim to feel a kind of kinship with him. He teases Elric by showing him Zarozinia, captive but unharmed. Moorcock describes the dead god as ape-like but oddly beautiful. I chose the colorful mandrill as inspiration for Darnizhaan's design.

Elric promises to give up the blades in exchange for his wife. The god, anticipating the unholy power that will be his to command, takes the blades in his enormous paws and gloats, "Ah, Elric, you've saved the world from a much duller age than this one!"

But as Zarozinia runs to his arms, Elric nods at Dyvim and the two cousins call out to their swords. Instantly Stormbringer and Mournblade turn on the shrieking Darnizhaan, ripping him to cosmic shreds. Below, the awestruck heroes watch (page 78), bathed in the rainbow glow (achieved by different colored gels over the camera lens) of the god's destruction. *Schertzo Fantastique* pounds to its sudden conclusion as we zoom in on Elric, Zarozinia and Dyvim's faces.

Immediately we cut to the Hall of Nihrain where Elric and his friends return to rest and get some answers. Moorcock's description of the immensity and unguessable age of this mountain fastness contains strong images easily translated into visuals. I attempted to evoke the atmosphere of a cavernous Egyptian tomb but without specific reference to any known culture. On the scale of this painting the walking figures would be about as big as grains of rice.

79

While an exhausted Zarozinia sleeps, Sepiriz gently informs Elric that the end of the world, as they know it, is at hand and that a new age is about to begin. Softly underscoring the narrated conversation is a selection from Diamond's *Romeo and Juliet* entitled "Romeo and Friar Lawrence." The music is a dialog of two opposing themes, one churchly and implacable, the other worldly and entreating.

▼ Elric listens, dreading to ask the question that burns within him.

► The camera frames a circular, backlit window, the symbolism of which will be echoed quite meaningfully at the end of the film, and pans down to a long shot of the sorcerer and the seer limned in ruddy light. Elric asks, "What part do the runeswords play in all this?" Sepiriz responds with pity, "The purpose of the blades is your destiny. They were meant to destroy this world."

▲ Elric recoils in horror, rejecting the responsibility. Although he agrees that the world and its gods are old, corrupt and ready for a cleansing, such an act would mean the obliteration of all that he knows and loves. ▶

Bearing the burden of this secret and terrible knowledge, Elric sails home to the City of Jade Towers with Zarozinia. Their warm but somber clothing is of Nihrainian design, given to them by Sepiriz. Zarozinia senses, without understanding why, that Elric is lost to her already. She cannot reach him and knows, somehow, that the black sword will never hang in the armory again.

At this point my heart went out entirely to the characters. I put my own feelings into Zarozinia's expression as she looks up at her doomed lord. Those are my eyes — were my eyes — at twenty.

Elric has no choice. If he stands by and does nothing, the demons of Hell will win and Chaos, a state of permanent anarchy, will engulf the world forever. But if he opposes Chaos and destroys the very demons that he and all Melnibonéans have worshipped for thousands of years, an age of Law will come to the land. Men will at least be able to make their own destiny, free of the influence of evil — or good — gods. Either way, Elric's fate is sealed.

This realization finally pushes the albino sorcerer over the edge. Since he, his world and his gods are doomed, Elric decides simply to enjoy the fireworks. But first he vows to destroy Jagreen Lern, pawn of Chaos, upstart human wizard who seeks to emulate the conquering Melnibonéan ancients.

◄ I disliked the clichéd device of the magic mirror but decided to use it because it irked me to have the narration refer to a character who was not somehow visually included in the scene. Now I am more forgiving of myself and have come to appreciate the allegory of the glass in which the hero sees the villain, the dark side of himself, reflected.

◄ Lost now, existing only in test footage, a few cels of dialog animation are based on this profile shot of Elric stroking the blade and saying, "Come, old friend." Much as it embarrassed me, a faithful interpretation of Moorcock's story, I knew, had to acknowledge the blatant phallic symbolism. I chose this point in the film to do so. If Elric was going a little mad, so was I.

Accompanied this time by Moonglum, rather than by Dyvim, Elric gallops away to find Jagreen Lern. The music is the dashing "Allegro Molto" from Rachmaninov's *Symphony No. 2 in E Minor, Opus 27*.

The camera pans from upper left to lower right in this up-angle shot, creating the illusion that the magic horse is flying offscreen, frame left.

◄ Elric and Moonglum land on the shore of Pan Tang, Jagreen Lern's island stronghold. There they are met by ferocious "watch-griffins." But Elric, still high on nihilism, laughs a few sorcerous words and the beasts slink away.

Next the albino and his friend are attacked by an army of warrior priests who daunt Moonglum. Elric, however, relishes the feast of souls, laying into the attackers and slaughtering them to a man. ►

89

That is how, to paraphrase Moorcock, Elric and Moonglum came to enter the City of Screaming Statues in some style. The background music for this scene is an excerpt from the percussive *Burlesque Overture* by Francis Thorne.

▲ The high wall surrounding Jagreen Lern's capital city is lined with thousands of stone figures, each containing the living soul of one of the wizard's victims. The cries of eternal torment issuing from the statues are meant to warn away all intruders. Elric ignores them —

— and issues his challenge by destroying a shrine which contains the bones of Jagreen Lern's ancestors. It is not the wizard who appears to take up the gauntlet, but those he has summoned: Xiombarg, Mabelrode and even Arioch, Archduke of Hell, Elric's own patron demon.

A continuing theme throughout the story is that of imagerial beauty masking infinite evil. Arioch is described as androgynous, overwhelmingly lovely and irresistibly seductive. At a loss as to how to represent him, all I could do was ask myself, "What would get to me? What would I be unable to resist?" I figured it had to be a chimerical creature that could become, at will, my heart's desire of the moment. But how to consolidate those shifting qualities into one being?

◀ My less than satisfactory solution was to rely on color. Arioch is a hodgepodge of patterns and hues suggestive of Chaos, symbolized by the eight-pointed emblem he wears on his brow. A standard "come hither" facial expression makes the demon more laughable than menacing.

Because I wasn't trying so hard, I had better luck with the design of Arioch's companion Xiombarg. This demon seems more unearthly, less easy to read. ▶

The Dukes of Hell try to lure Elric over to the cause of Chaos, promising him anything he desires. But all Elric wants is peace. He casts a spell to call down Stormbringer's brothers. The sky fills with screaming black swords that rain down on the Dukes, destroying forever their earthly forms. Overcome with the horror of it, Elric and Moonglum collapse.

When Elric awakens to ominous chords from the first movement of Rachmaninov's *Symphony No. 2* he finds himself stripped bare, a prisoner, without Stormbringer to lend him its supernatural strength. The black sword vanished with its brothers when the demons were destroyed.

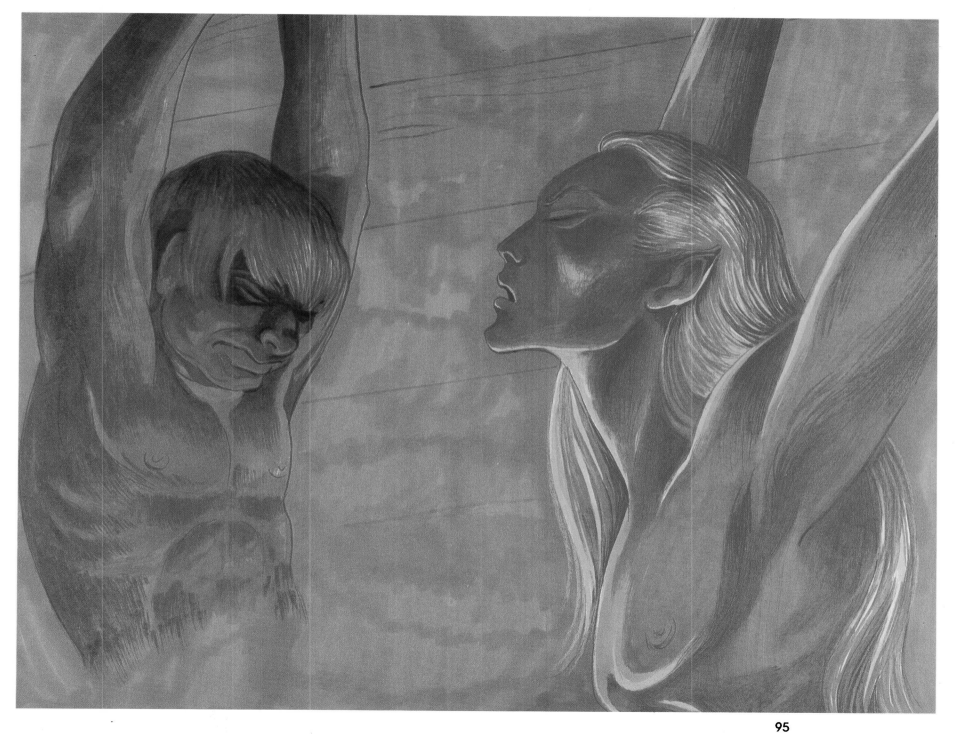

Jagreen Lern takes terrible revenge on Elric and Moonglum, torturing them with fire in the hold of his armada's flagship (page 95). Days later the wizard orders a near-dead Elric brought up on deck where he will be forced to watch the destruction of his allies who are manning the southern fleet. After that, Jagreen Lern promises, comes the capture of Karlaak — and Zarozinia. ▶

The shot of Elric lashed to the mast while Jagreen Lern taunts him (page 97) is one of the best composed drawings in the film. I was finally beginning to understand the value of negative space. The judiciously placed rigging which crosses Elric's groin was intended to hide his nudity. But I apparently chickened out later and added a loincloth. My mixed feelings, during the project, about frankly depicting Elric's sexuality were never resolved. The inhibition came from over-identification with the character, from things I did not wish to reveal about myself, from sheer immaturity.

97

Never one to give up, despite his avowed fatalism, Elric goes into a trance and attempts to summon Stormbringer. Jagreen Lern orders him slain, but the black sword appears in the nick of time to cut Elric's bonds and feed him its power. With a rescued Moonglum slung over his shoulder Elric swims for the southern fleet where he is hauled aboard by none other than Dyvim Slorm.

◄ The two armadas engage but Jagreen Lern's powerful sorcery prevails. Elric and Dyvim have no chance to use the runeswords to aid their allies, for Sepiriz appears and whisks them away with Moonglum in a magical golden globe. Sepiriz tells the frustrated swordsmen that they dare not waste their energies in battles they cannot win. Because of Jagreen Lern's conjurings, chaos has come to the earth and soon will engulf it.

► Tired, wounded, despairing, the three heroes see no hope for the world's future. Chaos cannot be fought because it warps everything it touches. However, in his usual cryptic manner Sepiriz suggests that all may not be lost. The golden globe heads for the Fortress of Evening on the Island of the Purple Towns.

And who should be waiting for Elric in that place of rest and healing but his loving wife.

◀ The camera pans left from Elric's startled profile and zooms out to include a full figure shot of Zarozinia. A color model done in elongated fashion-drawing style shows the minute detail of Elric's unusual costume. Since he wouldn't be wearing it in any other scenes, I let him indulge himself in a little sartorial extravagance.

Sepiriz had Zarozinia brought to the fortress for safety, and also because of his compassion for the long-separated lovers. To the pleading violin strains of "Le Prince et La Princesse" from Prokofiev's *Suite from The Love for Three Oranges* Elric and Zarozinia quarrel(▲). It is easier to do that than face the knowledge that they must soon part again. At last they fall into each others' arms. ▶

◄ Next morning a trumpet announces a new arrival at the fortress.

I liked making ordinary things like a mirror, a wash basin or a dresser look a little unworldly while still retaining their functionality. In this "morning after" shot I wanted to create a feeling of ordinary domesticity, something Elric and Zarozinia hadn't had too much of in recent times. The simplest, most familiar things — shaving, sunrise — take on poignant significance in the face of a cosmic crisis.

With forced cheerfulness the recovered friends greet each other. The ▼ newcomer is Rackhir the Red Archer, and old companion of Elric's from the mythical city of Tanelorn.

◄ A very gentle hero, a servant of Law is Rackhir. Of all my character designs for *Stormbringer* I think the Red Archer is the most sophisticated. Here personality wins over physical attractiveness. Kindness and beauty of spirit shine through the eyes. Rackhir is described as almost skeletal in his thinness. To me he seemed a man of arrows built like a single, upward pointing arrow, the symbol of Law.

Sepiriz tells the assembled heroes about the Sad Giant's Shield, the only thing in the universe that can withstand the warping influence of Chaos. With it a blow for Law can be struck, demons can be driven back to their own dimensions and no harm can come to the shield-bearer. But the shield must be won from its owner, Mordaga, a god-turned-mortal who lives far off in the Sighing Desert.

RACKHIR THE RED ARCHER

◄ After a harrowing journey, the four men arrive at Mordaga's castle. The stairs to the entrance are lined with elder trees which contain the imprisoned souls of gods. Murderously, the elders lash out at the intruders. Elric and Dyvim plunge their swords deep into the writhing timber, absorbing the extreme power of the gods.

▲ Moonglum and Rackhir hang back, afraid of what Elric and Dyvim have become. Like two fiends from hell the cousins butcher Mordaga's armed guards, killing and killing until long after it is necessary. When Rackhir, out of pity, tries to stop the massacre he too, like so many other friends of Elric, falls victim to Stormbringer's lust (page 108). Mordaga is also slain and the shield is taken, but at a terrible price.

◄ The death of Rackhir, a sacrificial lamb if ever there was one, truly depressed me. I found myself for once at odds with the material, saying "enough is enough!" Perhaps that is one reason why the artwork covering the remaining scenes of the story is so sparse and scattershot. It became very difficult to cope with the deaths of so many characters that I cared about. High tragedy is uplifting, and I will not deny that I got a perverse thrill from the intense morbidity of the story, but the last section of the novel entitled "Doomed Lord's Passing" is absolutely relentless.

▲ Now captain of the Chaos Fleet, vile, corrupting ships of the dead that flow on land as well as water, Jagreen Lern has taken a defiant Zarozinia prisoner. The wizard knows Elric will come for her and cannot wait to destroy him.

Protected by the Chaos Shield, Elric boards the flagship, slaying the fleet's overlord, the tentacled demon Pyaray. As the chaos ships dissolve into pestilent muck, Jagreen Lern is forced to flee for his life, but not before he has his revenge.

▶ Elric finds Zarozinia, hideously transformed, in one of the cabins. I thought it would heighten the horror to show the outlines of her once lovely body beneath the white worm's flesh, but somehow the image is less gruesome because of that choice.

Sobbing, Zarozinia throws herself on Stormbringer's point so that her soul may mingle with Elric's. He screams, and all around him abstract images of nature gone mad begin to swirl as though going down a drain.

I found an especially good theme for the Chaos Fleet and Pyaray in "Scene Infernale" from Prokofiev's *Suite*. The music lumbers ponderously, its rising minor chords suggesting the unstoppable approach of a juggernaut.

For Zarozinia's death, "Scene Infernale" blends with a tempestuous passage from the "Adagio" from Albert Roussel's *Symphony No. 3 in G Minor*. This music, inspired by the sea, builds to a heartbreaking crescendo, then grows soft and mournful.

▲ Elric rejoins his companions, all hope and spirit gone. I rendered the scene in pencil gray to give it a desolate feel.

The three heroes retreat to the Dragon Isle of Melniboné, the only place in the world that Chaos has not yet touched. The sun stands in the sky at high noon, awaiting Elric's next move. But the albino sorcerer is tired and sickened with grief. Whatever force keeps him from taking his own life is not strong enough to lift him out of his lethargy. He dreams of Zarozinia, he broods, he mourns.

As Elric sleeps, Sepiriz visits him in astral form and carries his spirit through multiple dimensions to meet the Lords of Law. The ethereal "Neptune" from Gustav Holst's *The Planets* musically sets the scene.

I got very excited about this sequence, not just for its visual possibilities, but for its philosophical content as well. It is here on the plane of Law that Elric realizes the importance of the Cosmic Balance. Both Law and Chaos, acting in harmony, are necessary for progress. If either side dominates, stagnation results.

This dovetailed neatly with my own thoughts, which I still espouse, about the nature of creativity. In a state of total tranquility, the artist is not motivated to work. Tension, "eustress," disorder of some kind is necessary for the sparks of inspiration to fly.

The radiant Lords of Law, symmetrical and serene, approach garbed for battle. ▶

There were no such things as glitter pens back then, just good old Elmer's glue, a package of sparkles and luck. I had seen glitter filmed wonderfully through a star filter in a 1961 Japanese animated film *Alakazam the Great* and wanted to emulate the effect.

◄ After all he has been through, Elric has no respect left for god or man. He is fed up with being the tool of destiny and bluntly asks the Lords of Law what they want him to do. The Lords command him to obtain the Horn of Fate, a mystical instrument which belongs to Roland, a hero of another age. Elric must blow the horn three times: first to wake the Melnibonéan war dragons, second to summon the Lords of Law to earth, and third to herald the end of the world.

► Elric does capture the horn from Roland and returns with it to his own Chaos-plagued time. He tells Moonglum and Dyvim of his adventure and leads them to the dragon caves under the ruined towers of Imrryr. Here the ominous, ever-building notes of Holst's "Saturn, the Bringer of Old Age" hint that something awesome is about to occur.

The dragons have slept for centuries, but the first blast of the Horn of Fate rouses them. The effort takes nearly all of Elric's strength. He realizes he is dying, but feels strangely calm, speaking affectionately to the lead dragon Flamefang (page 118).

Elric, Moonglum and Dyvim lead a flight of the venom-spewing creatures right into the heart of Chaos, "For Melniboné and vengeance!"

During the battle, Dyvim Slorm is sent hurtling down in flames (page 119). Elric stands over his slain cousin's body and blows the Horn of Fate a second time (page 120).

As they had promised, the Lords of Law answer the ordained summons and enter the earth plane. Shimmering, ecstatic, "Lolli's Pursuit of the Evil God and Sunrise" from *Scythian Suite* underscores a colossal battle between Law and Chaos. However, just as in their first meeting, Elric and Jagreen Lern have their final duel apart from the conflict raging around them. Abandoned, no longer of use to the demons he thought he commanded, Jagreen Lern is no match for even a dying Elric. ▶

▲ It takes the wizard an hour to perish, and only then because Moonglum begs the smiling, abstracted Elric to finish him quickly. Again, I put my personal emotions into a drawing. Jagreen Lern's is the one death in the story that I savored.

121

The battle subsides. Elric and Moonglum are left standing alone on a vast, featureless plain. But the triumph of Law cannot be complete, for Elric hasn't the strength to blow the Horn a final time. In a last act of friendship, Moonglum sacrifices himself to the black sword, feeding Elric the bit of power he needs. The (in retrospect) too-heavy background music is from the middle of the first movement of Franck's *Symphony in D Minor*.

When the last clear, sad note of the Horn finally fades, Elric witnesses the rising of a new dawn's sun (▲) and knows that his efforts have not been in vain. It is then that Stormbringer turns upon him and takes his soul. He falls beside the friend who had been with him from the beginning and was there, faithfully, at the end. ◄

The blade assumes its true form and whispers, "Farewell, friend. I was a thousand times more evil than thou."

For the transmutation of sword to demon I painted two identical drawings of Elric, one with the bloody blade hovering over him (►) and the other, a cut-out of just Elric and the demon (page 124) designed to be laid directly over the figures in the first painting. By simply dissolving from one shot the the other, the onscreen transformation and color change is achieved.

To the stirring climax of "Allegro non Troppo," again from *Symphony in D Minor*, the laughing sword-demon streaks toward the heavens, ready to keep the Cosmic Balance from tipping too far in favor of Law.

124

Even in death, Elric knows that he will have no peace, for he is the Eternal Champion, maintainer of the Balance, doomed to return again and again under different names to the battlefield, earth.

The final image before fadeout is that of the new dawn. The sun, like the red stained-glass window in Sepiriz's quarters, looks down on the promise of a fresh beginning.

On the night in October 1973 that I decided to lay the Stormbringer film to rest, I tore up a particularly elaborate backdrop, just to see if I could do it, sealed off the door to my studio in our Watertown, Massachusetts flat and didn't go back in for several days. Richard was very solicitous and a little scared. Suddenly the juggernaut artist had been replaced by a vulnerable human being. For me it was like trying to kick a drug habit. The emptiness, the sense of loss, of failure, paralyzed me. But beneath that pain stirred a kind of relief which I was later able to own without guilt. Richard and I both knew it was time to move on to other things — and we did. In later years Richard's career as planetarium director/teacher and mine as cartoonist/illustrator overlapped frequently as we worked together on many new ventures. In 1978 when we developed, produced and published our *Elfquest* comics series, we fused into the kind of creative team that had not been possible with the *Stormbringer* film. Elfquest's swift success and positive audience reception had much to do, I think, with the fact that it was the realization of my personal vision rather than an interpretation of someone else's story. Nevertheless, some four hundred pieces of art, the choicest of which you have seen in this volume, remain as evidence of a five-year commitment to an impossible dream. I do not consider that a failure.

In 1976 I met Michael Moorcock for the first and, as yet, only time at the World Fantasy Convention in New York City. He was still shaken by hours of travel, which he said he disliked intensely, and seemed shy and reserved. Of the *Stormbringer* artwork that I had on display in his honor his guarded comment was that it struck him as "over-romanticized." Moorcock had once written me that he himself was Elric. At the time I had found that hard to credit since the author reputedly had the size and appearance of a Viking. But upon meeting him in person I realized that he had laid much of his soul bare on paper and was, perhaps, somewhat embarrassed by it. Elric's self-deprecating humor and charm were there in the flesh. For a moment the world of the senses and the theater-of-the-mind movie became one.   ✳

(Next page) My farewell painting and thought on the entire subject — entitled, appropriately, "The Universe **Is** Just!"